CW00853800

THE RAMBLINGS OF JOHN W. WOOD

Poems and Short Stories

JOHN W. WOOD

I dedicate this book of poems and short stories to my friend and fellow Veteran, James Spears. James, also known as Boats, is the founder of the US NAVY SALTY DOGS, a private online site of 52,759 Navy men and women who come together and tell their tales of the sea. James also does something else; he has dedicated himself to visit terminally ill veterans who are alone or in need. James does this mostly on his dime with the occasional help of a few. He is my friend and has been of great help to me in my writing. I wanted to honor him in some way, and this book is it.

Semper Fi, James, I love you brother

To The Reader

At nearly eighty years of age, my past often comes back to me in flashes. On occasion, it inspires a poem, something I cannot seem to write on command. But most of the time my memories develop into short stories. I write them down and then file them away. My partner Mary Felix read a few and convinced me to put them together into a book. You'll meet Mary as you read, I love her dearly, and she has been my inspiration over the years. As a Marine, Police Officer, and a man hired to protect others, I have seen and experienced a great deal. I have tried to share some of these experiences in this book of Ramblings.

Some Must Go

I'm the boy from down the street
I'm the one you thought so sweet
I'm the boy who said, "Good morning, Ma'am."
I'm the one who held the door, who mowed
    your lawn
I'm the one who went when none would go
I'm the one and many more, who went to war
I'm the one with dreams of life who jumped from
    planes
I'm the one who climbed the nets
I'm the one who drove the tanks and sailed the
    ships
We're the ones who'll not come home

Betrayed

Leaning upon his mighty sword, he stood Guard
Eyeing the horizon for signs of trouble
His armor scarred and dented from battle after
*   battle*
But it wasn't an enemy seen and fought that
*   brought him down*
But the black shaft of ignorance and deceit that
*   pierced his armor*
And then his heart

The Green Machine

You know we do not come in peace!
But you told us there was no other choice
You called, and we obeyed
Advancing through the fog of war
We Marines; the Green Machine
We do not come in peace!

The Gates of Hell

Night and day the big guns roared flames and
     cordite smoke filled the air
The dawn is dark the morning chill bone-deep
A metal voice commands, "Coxswains, man your
     boats!"
Winches scream and hearts they race the sea is
     chop the shore is near
Armed men stand in silent fear their packs are
     heavy legs are weak
The rope netting laid or the side down below our
     gray metal ride
The metal voice speaks once again, "Marines,
     man, your boats!"
The smell of diesel, shuffling feet hands are strong
     but somehow weak
Creaking rope-net beneath our feet upturned
     faces watch our descent
The metal deck rises, the net goes slack, boots hit
     the side, a foot is caught!

Quick thinking hands pull it taught boots on the
    deck, safe for now
Now we circle, circle, waiting, waiting
Coxswains push the throttles full the spray wets
    us all as the decks rise and fall
"Stand-by," a voice shouts out our heats nearly
    giving out
Then we are there; the ramp comes down, the
    coxswains good we'll not drown
"Follow me," the Lieutenant yells and leads us
    through to the gates of hell

The Gentle Man

A gentle-man they all agreed
He walked for miles, did you know?
Rain or shine and in the snow
Always pleasant with a smile, a nod, "Hello."
What makes a man so gentle they would ask?
But the answer they would never know
Of ribbons with metal stars pinned in a row
Across his chest by men who know
That this gentle-man had lost his mind in a war
    fought long ago
His friends had died to save his life
His vengeance flared
If he lived or died, he didn't care
He charged the enemy; he killed them all
In that far off place, that forgotten hell
He couldn't sleep, he couldn't rest
The daemons came they called his name
But he remembered his friends now cold
Who had fought for him, freedom and their
    homes

So he walked and walked mile after mile
He did not want to be what he had been
He beat the daemons he began to smile
He became the gentle-man that no one knew

Join The Navy

We were boys, not quite men
We got in trouble now and then
Then one day while in town
A man asked, "Son, have you been around?"
"We've been nowhere," we did expound
"Well," said he, "You should join the Navy!"
There are places both warm and cold
With exotic women and they're bold
Why son they'll sweep you clean off your feet!
All you need do is join the fleet
Go to sea and save the world.
We stood as men and took the pen
They smiled and welcomed us aboard
Handed us a swab, a broom, and pan
Told us, "clean up boys, become a man!"
We soon longed for home, to be a boy
But something happened along the way
The boys began to learn a lot
Mechanical things and those damned knots
We broke our knuckles complained a lot

We thought ourselves a sorry lot
Then one day the sea grew black sky was gray
That great hunk of iron began to sway!
We hadn't time for fear to come
We hit the decks on the run
When daylight came, we still were there
No longer boys for we were crew, and each one of
*   us knew*
Navy men, each and every one, proud of what
*   we'd become*

My Valentine

We met late in life
We both had tried love and failed
But something clicked, when we met
We fell in love
Had we met earlier we agreed it would have
*   failed*
But I often wish I had more time
To love my Mary, my Valentine

Autumn Love

It was our autumn when we met
Our love full of color like autumn leaves
An Indian summer for us both
Winters come, there'll be no spring
Your bloom, your warmth is gone; I miss you so
If you cannot be with me, then I will come to be
*   with you*

Someday

Do you remember as a kid all the things we said,
the things we did?
Not understanding what our parents said, "When
you grow up you'll understand"
About making noise, climbing branches, daring
each to take chances
Climbing roofs and then jumping, throwing
snowballs at the cars
Climbing fences, ringing doorbells in the night
Getting caught all full of fright
Now we're older, and we wonder why our kids
don't listen
To what is said, "When you grow up, you'll
understand."

Forever

Found upon a temple wall written in an ancient
*   scrawl*
A boy of a distant time etch of his broken heart
His scratched-in words told how his love for her
Would live forever though she had taken another
*   lover*
Leaving him alone to write upon this temple wall

I Wanted You To Know

We have talked, you and me
Of what to do if one must leave
We've talked of money, home and kids
Whom to call.... who would care
But while I can, I want you to know
How much I love you, how much I care
For all you've done and for your support
For loving me with all my warts
Accepting my apologizes for things I've done
You are my life you are the ONE
I wanted you to know before one of us must go

I'm A Cowboy!

Saturday Matinee They ride
Wild Bill Elliot and Randolph Scott
Out of the dark into the sun
Home again on the run I get my silver gun
Back outside, I've got no hat, I've got no chaps
Slapping my leg, off I go on my imaginary horse,
   Ringo
My sidekicks are Wild Bill and Randolph Scott,
Both of them I like a lot
We see the bad guys, there they go!
But they're no match for my Ringo
Scott and Elliot both ride up
Scott, his voice is deep, "Good job, son, you're the
   best."
Elliot's bright white smile tells me the rest
You're one of us. You are a cowboy!

A Fickle Mistress

I am a writer, I write for myself and the pure joy of the story. My characters based on people I know or whom I have met. The plots come from history I have read or the pleasure and pain of the life I have lived. I agonize when I cannot write. Writing is a demanding mistress, laying guilt trips upon me when I'm away. When I do return, she talks incessantly telling me story after story. But she can be a bitch. If I stay away too long, she will refuse to speak to me, turning a cold shoulder to my desire to write, seeming to delight in my frustration.

But I love her, and I come back, time after time until she relents, and the story flows once again.

Soap Box

We are a nation of different kinds
Different colors, different race
Different languages, different face
You'll hear us cry you'll hear us whine
We stand on boxes that once held soap
We raise our voices to shout our hope
Some will listen some will not
Many think us a crazy lot
But it is our right, something new
To speak our minds without fear

The Writer

I sometimes look back, and it is hard to believe
*   how far I have traveled*
The many people that I have met, the many
*   places I have seen*
The joy and pain of life experienced, the goodness
*   and evil I have seen*
Battles I have won or lost, the joy and sadness
*   brought by both*
The loves and hates I have experienced or caused
Sometimes I question why I have seen and done
*   so much*
But then, I pick up my pen, and I begin to write
*   and write*
The past leading the way

Dementia

A muddled memory of today
That seems so far away
But my history seems brand new
Of Baby birds and cowboy things
Garden snakes and magic rings
Secret places in a bush or tree
Blue skies and bumblebees
Bikes and skates scraped up knees
And then it fades...just like today

Writing

There is something mystical to writing
When a writer places their thoughts and feelings
Upon a page, so others
Might look at what they have seen and heard
  or felt
And later, when the writer's life has passed
Perhaps someone will read his words and be
  touched
By what he wrote, long ago

The Warrior

Today a wreath was laid at my marker, and I
proclaimed a warrior, a young man who gave
his life for God and country
I received medals I will never wear and was
praised by those I'll never meet
It is said that my deeds and valor will be
remembered
But when all is said and done, I would have
rather been remembered as a husband and a
father
But then, someone had to go

Smelling Like a Rose

My name is Bird. Lance Corporal Bird United States Marine Corps. I was in a guard company with one of the luckiest guys I ever met. His name was Swift, PFC J.W. Swift. It was 1960, on one of those jungle-covered outcroppings of coral in the middle of the Pacific Ocean.

I liked Swift; he was a good Marine. But he was full of mischief; I don't think a month of our tour went by; he wasn't standing before the Man explaining himself. But more often than not, he'd come out smelling like a rose. Take, for instance, that night he and Bishop got in a gunfight. I shit you not! A shootout! Let me tell you about it.

The armory was a room ten feet long by six feet wide. It had two wall lockers with padlocks where the ammunition and weapons were stored. PFC Swift, the company armorer, stood at the bench, working on a Colt .45 automatic. One of the Marines on guard duty had been practicing fast draw and fumbled it. The hammer spur broke off, and Swift was replacing the hammer. Swift damned near dropped the pistol again; someone was banging on the locked metal door of the armory. Swift went to the door and yanked it open.

PFC Bishop stood in the doorway. "What the hell, Man! Are you trying to give me a heart attack or something?" Asked Swift, angrily. "I thought you were on patrol."

"Fuck man, there are lights near the West Tower. I got trespassers." That perked Swift up; trespassers were probably poachers after deer or wild pigs. Fresh meat was scarce for the villagers on the island, and the best hunting was on the Naval Magazine. There was one problem with that, actually two. One, you had to have a secret clearance just to stand the main gate and greet visitors. Second, there were explosives stored out there. It was a standing joke that if the magazine ever blew up, the Earth would look like an apple with a bite out of it, a great big bite.

"I'm afraid that if I make contact and fire my weapon, they'll send me to the brig. That asshole First Sergeant is just itching to bust someone so he can show his brass balls to the troops."

The asshole First Sargent was First Sergeant Ferguson, the new company First Shirt. We heard he was the youngest Marine promoted to the rank. He had just taken everyone on a five-mile night run when he found a toothpick in "His" G. I. Can. The problem was he felt he had to arm himself on the run because Ferguson realized he had pushed the men too far. Now he was on the hunt to make someone an example.

Swift never hesitated, "What are you carrying?" He asked as he went to the weapons locker.

"I got a pistol and a shotgun."

Opening the locker, Swift pulled out his pistol belt and holster. He took a forty-five and two loaded magazines and laid them on the workbench. Going back to the locker, he brought out a Model 12 shotgun and ten brass shot-shells. He then locked the cabinets and turned to Bishop, "Let's go."

"You're going with me? Can you do that? I mean, hell, man, you ain't even on the roster!"

Swift got a lopsided smile on his face; a smile most of the Marines had learned meant something was going to hit the fan. "Don't worry about it. The Sergeant of the Guard is out checking posts, and the Officer of the Day is the new Navy Ensign who still needs someone to tie his shoes."

Swift pushed the pistol into the holster and looped the belt over his shoulder. He picked up the shotgun and shells and began pushing Bishop out of the room and into the hallway. In the hall, he turned closed the door and then made sure it was locked. "Truck out in front?" Bishop nodded his head, yes.

As Swift and Bishop started for the Gray Navy pickup truck, another patrol truck pulled up. "Oh shit, whispered Bishop, "It's the Officer of the Day."

Swift saw that the O.D. was with Chief Boatswain Mate Carter. Both Swift and Bishop saluted the O.D. "Good evening, sir." The Marines said in unison.

"Good evening," The Officer replied, returning the salute.

Boats, a ten year veteran of the Navy, had that Popeye look on his face, one eye kinda closed, his head tilted and his fists on his hips. He knew Swift and knew what he was capable of. "What are you two up to?" He asked.

Bishop looked like he was going to piss his shorts when Swift, with feigned urgency in his voice, said, "Trespassers near the West Tower. Bishop saw their lights; we're on our way to intercept them."

Boats stood straight up; his eyes seemed to shine in the dark, "We got agents in a restricted area?" The O.D. looked uncomfortable. He knew about the crazy Marines at the Naval Magazine, and here he was with two them armed to the teeth. Now he wasn't too sure about Boatswain Mate Carter, who looked like he'd was invited to a beer bust.

The O.D. turned to Carter and asked, "What's the West tower?"

"It's a fire tower; use to have a fire watch up there, but with the Marine patrols now, we stopped using it."

"Sir," said Swift, "If you and Boats drove to the West tower and waited, Bishop and I will drive to the area where he saw the lights. There's a firebreak that runs right up to the tower. We'll blink our lights, and you can work your way down to the area where Bishop saw the lights. We'll try and catch them between us."

The O.D. looked unsure of himself. He was also more than a little peeved that a Marine PFC was making suggestions to an officer. But then Boats said, "Sounds like a good idea. If the agents are still there, they'll not want to go crashing off into the jungle at night. Hell Sir, no one's ever caught a trespasser before."

The O.D. immediately took the bait, thinking he might get points with the Old Man if, on his first duty night, he captured agents in a restricted area. He decided to follow the PFC's suggestion. "We'll head for the tower, and wait for your lights. Key your radio mike twice, and we'll start down."

"Aye, aye Sir," The Marines responded and headed for their patrol truck.

Five minutes later, Bishop turned out the vehicle lights and pulled off the paved road onto the firebreak. The full moon made the coral firebreak seem to glow in the dark. Thick jungle pressed in like a wall on both sides of the break. Bishop stopped the truck. "See that bend in the road? Just to the left of that hill is where I saw the lights."

Swift saw that there was a hill on the left side of the firebreak. "Let's wait here for Boats and the O.D. to start down," said Swift.

The two Marines sat in the truck with the windows down listening. It didn't take long for the mosquitos to find them. "You got the spray," asked Swift.

"In the glove compartment," replied Bishop. The spray was DDT in a green spray can. Every Marine that had night duty carried a can. The Marines joked that the mosquitos were big enough to drag a man off into the brush and suck him dry of blood. Swift sprayed the palms of his hands until there was a pool of DDT, and then he closed his eyes and applied it to his face and neck. He then sprayed his uniform and handed the can to Bishop, who did the same.

"I wonder where the hell the O.D. is," asked Bishop.

Swift opened the door of the truck. "I'm going to stand in the bed of the truck. Maybe I'll be able to see further up the break." With that, he got out and laid his shotgun on the floorboard of the truck. Outside, Swift climbed into the bed of the truck. Then standing behind the cab, he searched for the lights of the other vehicle.

The humming and biting of the mosquitos were becoming unbearable. Swift ran his hand over his face. He saw dead bugs rolled up in a bloody mess in the palm of his hand. Jumping down from the bed of the truck, Swift spoke to Bishop. "I'm going to walk up the break to that curve. Got to get away from these damned bugs; give me the portable-radio just in case I need you to move. The portable was cumbersome, but it gave the Marines communications if they had to get out of the patrol vehicles.

Bishop watched as Swift moved up the firebreak and then disappeared around the bend. Swift had no sooner gone out of sight when all hell broke loose. Bishop heard, "Halt, halt!" Then there were shots.

That's a fucking rifle, thought Bishop. And then he heard the distinctive pop, pop of a forty-five. "Ah fuck me, we're both going to the fucking brig," Bishop said aloud. Grabbing the radio mike on the dash of the truck, he keyed the mike. "Girth Hitch Sierra, Girth Hitch Sierra, this is Poppa one. My location is firebreak twelve. Shots fired, shots fired." Bishop didn't wait for a response. He grabbed his shotgun and began running towards the gunfire.

Swift was lying off to the side of the firebreak on his stomach. Bishop thought Swift was shot. But then he saw the pistol in the Marine's hand pointed at the hill. "Over here, take cover!" Swift yelled at him.

Bishop heard a pop, pop, as he hit the ground next to Swift. Swift pointed at the hill, "Shoot them fuckers, he yelled." Bishop pumped the shotgun and pulled the trigger, "click." He pumped it again, "click."

Swift snatched the gun from Bishop's hands and began examining it. "Look here he said, pointing with his finger at the magazine tube. "It's got a dent in it, and the shells won't feed."

"I must have banged it on the truck window when I got out," said Bishop.

"Marine, you're gonna die shouted a voice out of the jungle."

Swift and Bishop looked at each other, "You gotta be shitten me; someone has been watching too many war movies," said Swift. He pointed his pistol at the hill and fired off two shots into the dark. The response was the crack of a rifle and a limb falling on the heads of the two Marines.

Then from the direction of the paved road, they could hear a truck, and then it stopped, and someone got out. "Here comes the cavalry," said Swift.

"We're going to the brig. We'll never catch those fuckers,

and the First Sergeant will think we were just screwing around," whined Bishop.

The cavalry came in the form of a pissed-off Marine named Lemkin. He came strolling up the firebreak his M-1 rifle held in his left hand. "Swift, you fucker, you got me out of a sound sleep. You are in deep shit; everyone at the barracks is pissed."

The ground around Lemkin's feet began to explode as bullets hit the coral. Lemkin, now fully awake, ran and jumped off the firebreak. He grabbed the mike of the portable radio and said, "Help! They're fucking shooting at us!"

I don't think that's proper radio procedure," said Swift calmly. "You'll probably get in trouble over that," With that Bishop and Swift burst into laughter while a wild-eyed Lemkin looked at them as if they were nuts.

The portable crackled, and a voice said, Poppa One, Poppa One, this is Girth Hitch Sierra.

Lemkin keyed the mike just as someone fired off an automatic weapon. The coral bounced and ricocheted into the air around the three Marines.

Back at the Sergeant of the Guard's office, the Sergeant of the Guard, the First Sergeant and the Company Commander, Lieutenant Smith, heard the gunfire over the radio. "They don't have automatic weapons," said Smith, "Those men are under fire!"

The Sergeant of the Guard turned and punched a button on the office wall. Red lights in the barracks began spinning as a siren started blaring. Sleeping, Marines sprang from their bunks and began dressing. Within three and a half minutes, they were armed and running out the door to waiting trucks. The cavalry was on its way.

At the firebreak, all was quiet. "We're going to the brig;

you know that, don't you? Those guys are long gone, and we are going to the fucking brig!"

Swift's head came up," Listen, do you hear that?"

Trucks, four of them, three filled with Marines and one truck with six sailors who had heard the radio traffic pulled up. At the wheel of the fourth truck was Boats. The Officer of the Day sat next to him. It seems the Ensign had had second thoughts and had driven to the safety of the Navy office instead of to the West Tower. Boats heard the shots over the radio, and he dashed out of the office, the chagrin Ensign on his heels.

Swift stood up and moved quickly up to the truck with the Company Commander in it. Saluting, Swift said, Good evening Sir."

Returning the salute, Smith demanded, "What the hell is going on here, Swift?"

"Sir, Bishop observed lights on that hill over there; we came to check it out when I came under fire."

First Sergeant Ferguson, looked skeptically at Swift. "And where did this happen?" Ferguson asked sarcastically.

"Right here, there's the heel of his shoe," replied Swift, pointing. Everyone looked. Sure enough, a heel from a boot lay on the firebreak. There was a groove made by a bullet running down the center of it.

One of the Marines picked it up and handed it to Lieutenant Smith, who looked expectantly at Swift.

Swift said, "I decided to walk up to the bend here and take a look. When I came around the bend, I saw a man in civilian clothing with a carbine in his hand; I ordered him to halt. He turned and fired at me and then started running. I fired two rounds at him with my pistol."

"Where did you fire from?"

"Right there at the bend," replied Swift.

Lieutenant Smith looked at the heel running his finger along the groove and then looked up at Swift. "Son, that's close to forty yards or so. With a forty-five, in the dark, at a running man who had just shot at you; that is mighty fine shooting."

A Marine walked up to the truck and said, "We have the lights, ready, sir."

The lights were two searchlights mounted in the bed of one of the trucks. As the men walked up to the lights, the Company Commander turned to Swift, "You say you think they were on that hill?"

"Yes, Sir," replied Swift.

The First Sergeant stepped up to the truck and retrieved a bullhorn from the bed of the truck. "Turn those lights on," he told a Marine standing by the lights. The lights were blinding when they came on and turned night into day. Ferguson stepped forward, and holding the bullhorn to his mouth pressed the trigger. There was a brief squeal, and then he spoke, "You men on the hill stand up with your hands on top of your heads, or we will open fire!"

From the back of the group of Marines, a voice could be heard whining, "We're going to the brig."

There was a moment of anticipation, but nothing happened. Ferguson turned to say something to Lieutenant Smith when a Marine said, "Well, kiss my ass."

Standing on the hill were five men, their hands on their heads. Lieutenant Smith gave a simple order, "Get em," and Marines moved up the hill to take them prisoner.

"What'd I tell you? One of the luckiest guys you'll ever meet. Swift wasn't even on the watch list! The next day, Ferguson wanted to have Swift court marshaled for the unauthorized issuing of firearms and firing his pistol! The

First Sergeant pleaded his case to the Lieutenant, but the L.T. just shook his head and held up some typed pages."

"See these? These are letters of accommodation from Fleet Marine Force Pacific for Swift and Bishop for prompt and courageous action while in a restricted area. I'm to make appropriate entries in their files. It isn't going to make anyone happy if I court-martial Swift; request denied."

"Ya see what I mean? That lucky bastard always came out smelling like a rose."

Loretta

It was 1917 in a small Michigan town, a very dull place for a girl of fourteen.

My father owned a working man's hotel located by the train depot. Lumberjacks, train crews, and traveling men stayed there while they were in town. I loved Dad's place; it had sleeping rooms upstairs with bunk beds built along the walls. The downstairs was one large room with dining tables, a bar, and a kitchen. A door at the back of the kitchen led into a room with a round card table surrounded by wooden captains' chairs. In a corner was a small potbellied stove, the stovepipe, a tin pipe that ran up the wall and out the roof. The room smelled of tobacco, cut wood, and men.

He was tall and handsome, with thick red hair and a full, black mustache. With his strong hands and long slender fingers, he could do magical things with a deck of cards.

Mother was as beautiful as my father was handsome. Raven-black hair and green eyes told of her Irish heritage. She adored Dad but was never afraid to speak her mind. She was an excellent cook, and the house always seemed to smell of fresh-baked bread.

That summer, my aunt Loretta, mother's younger sister, arrived from Detroit to live with us. She was twenty and had my mother's good looks.

Loretta was exciting; she came from the big city, had gone to concerts and plays. She knew how to dance, and we'd whirl around my room as she taught me how to dance. Like me, she read poetry and books, and we talked for hours.

Loretta enjoyed riding and often rode Dad's horse, Buck. She rode sidesaddle, wearing an emerald-green velvet dress and a small, cocked, black hat with a veil. She'd race across the fields, leaping the horse over fences. I was impressed but afraid of horses. My poor mother would be close to heart failure while Dad would smile and say, "She's quite a gal, your sister."

Indignant, Mother would look up at Dad, "Humph."

My bedroom located above the dining room, a register in the floor, allowed heat from the stove downstairs, into my room. Like the heat, voices also rose through the register. If I turned out the light and pulled a blanket over me, I could look down into the dining room without being seen. One night my mother and father were at the table talking.

"John, Mother asked, what are people to think of us?"

My Dad leaned toward her, patted her hand, "She's family; it doesn't matter what people think."

"But what about the father, why doesn't he make this right?

"I've sent Carl to Detroit to speak with him. In the meantime, we'll make her welcome."

Carl had served time in Joliet Prison after he killed a man in a fistfight years ago. He now worked for my father. He was a big, intimidating man who always wore a suit. Wherever Dad went, Carl was usually with him.

"What about Noreen, she's only fourteen, and she and Loretta spend much time together."

"Loretta and Noreen talk of books, poetry, and clothes; I think it's good she has Loretta to talk to."

By the time winter came, it had become evident that Loretta was pregnant.

Winter sometimes brought heavy snow that would block the trains. Then the train whistles would wail, calling for help. Townsmen would harness their horses to sleighs and head down the tracks to the snowbound train. Meanwhile, the wives would add wood to the cookstoves and get out extra blankets. The rescued passengers would be taken to the hotel or stay in private homes as guests until the snow could be removed from the track, and then the train would continue.

One winter night, I was in the living room with Loretta and my mother; we heard the stomping of feet on the front porch. Dad came in, brushing the snow from his shoulders. Through the open door, we heard the intermittent, shrill, of a train whistle.

"A train is snowbound about two miles out. I'm going with Mr. Passmore in his sleigh; we may have company."

Dad turned and left, closing the door behind him. We all got busy; I got out blankets, while mother went to the kitchen and began adding wood to the cookstove. Loretta, now quite pregnant, looked nervously about, and then went into the kitchen. I could hear her and mother talking, but I couldn't understand a word. Soon Loretta came out and went upstairs. Mother stood in the doorway of the kitchen, watching her climb the stairs. Then she noticed me.

"Let's get busy young lady; we have a lot to do."

Later, with a full silver moon to light their way, the rescuers returned. I heard the jingle of sleigh bells outside; I went to the window and looked out. Mr. Passmore was pulling up in his sleigh; Dad was sitting next to him. In the back of the sled were two people huddled in blankets. I rushed to the kitchen.

"Dad has two with him," I told mother.

Mother brushed back a strand of hair, smiled, "Not as bad as I thought."

The front door opened, and Dad and two men entered the house. The smell of tobacco and wet wool filled the entranceway. It took me a moment to realize that one of the men was Carl. The other, dressed in an Army uniform, was tall and broad-shouldered. His wide-brimmed campaign hat hid his face. There was a war on in Europe, and America had sent troops.

"Noreen, said Dad, help our guests with their coats and hats."

Carl handed me his coat and hat. As I reached for the soldier's coat, he removed his hat. I looked into blue eyes and a once handsome face. A scar, like a thin red rope, traveled from the corner of his mouth to his ear. I blinked; he winked and handed me his hat.

"Thank you," he said, as I took his hat.

"Noreen, show our guests into the living room; I'll be right in."

I led the two men into the living room and the warm stove. They were just taking their seats when my mother came in from the kitchen.

"Carl, when did you get back?"

"I was on the train, ma'am."

Mother began to speak but stopped; we all turned to look.

Dad and Loretta were entering the room. Behind me, I heard a chair scrape across the floor; I felt the soldier bushed past me. For a moment, he and Loretta stood frozen in place. Loretta's hand went to her mouth to stifle a cry. The soldier reached out and gently pulled into his embrace. Loretta's hands clutched at the back of his uniform as she wept.

"This is Lieutenant William Perry, announced Dad, who went to war planning to marry when he returned. However, he was wounded. He was in an Army Hospital where Carl found him."

It was late spring when William, Loretta, now married, and baby John moved to Chicago.

Over the years, we wrote to each other, but eventually, we lost touch. But occasionally, I'll read a book, or hear some music, and I'll remember Loretta. Loretta, who in her flight from shame, brought excitement into my life and taught me how to dance.

Cozy Cat

With tufts of hair between his toes
Furry pants against the cold
A small white mustache beneath his nose
Cozy Cat stretched out upon his back
His furry belly well exposed
So round so full so very fat
Cozy Cat

Forever

Forever; love, a vow, a place, a thing, a thought
Forever's pledged and then forgot
Forever said now but with more thought
Forever's not as long as it used to be

The Book

I'm sitting in a rocking chair on a screened-in porch, and the sounds of a humid Michigan night have dredged up memories. It's summertime, 1955, and late at night. I'm in my parent's house; the French windows next to my bed are open to let in some air. Crickets are singing acapella while June bugs with no rhythm at all, bounce off the window screens. My Dad is asleep in the other bedroom, and the house is dark, dark, except for a soft line of light seeping under the closed hallway door. I know she's out there; Mom will be sitting at the dining room table. A small table lamp her only illumination in that vast, dark room. Thin, but attractive, my mother has long, thick, black hair pulled back, held with bobby pins. She has large, expressive brown eyes above high cheekbones. I'm sure she's attractive because I've seen men look at her on the street, at least until they see her club foot. Then they look away. "Typhoid fever she tells people; a carrier came through town when I was a child. All the other children in town were vaccinated but me. My mother didn't believe in shots, and so I caught it." I will be full-grown when a family member tells me her father, my Grandpa, also had a club foot.

In the dining room, Mom's precious portable Royal typewriter sits on the dining room table. Surrounding it are the pages of her novel, some written in longhand, and some are typewritten. It is known only as "The Book." I can picture her cigarette resting in an ashtray, the smoke curling, drifting around the lamp like a conjured spirit. Mom is sitting on a straight-backed chair, leaning forward with one hand on the paper roller of the typewriter. Her teeth grip a yellow pencil while she reads what she has just written. If she likes what she has read, she'll cluck her tongue and then give a happy, "Ha!" But if she doesn't like it, the zzzz of the spinning gears of the paper-roller signals she has ripped the page from the typewriter. She'll then begin making changes to the offending page. Reading aloud, and then she'll stop to scribble notes in the margins or cross out words. Finished with her edits, she holds the offending page in her left hand while in her right hand, she holds the battered pencil ready to strike. As she scans the page, she absently places the pencil on the table and reaches for her cigarette. Nearly bringing the cigarette to her lips, she hesitates and then returns it to the ashtray, having never taken a puff of her smoke. As a new idea enters her mind, she will write on a blank paper in her flowing, looping cursive with a pencil. The story will once again flow from her head to that yellow, pocked marked Number two, and fill page after page. Then she'll stop, read, scribble, and then read some more. Later, the Royal will begin to click as she transcribes what she has written in longhand.

When Mom was a youngster, my Grandpa John would take her hunting and fishing. She loved him as only a girl can love a father. He was her hero, and she based many of the men in her stories on him.

Mom's life changed when her mother became ill and then lost her mind. It was a stressful and dangerous time because Grandma would sometimes hide behind a door and attack Mom with scissors or a sharpened pencil. An aunt who lived with them, was jilted by her lover, and attempted suicide with a pistol but failed. Though the wound was terrible, she lived for days with Mom taking care of both her and Grandma. Adding to her stress, my grandfather hired newly released convicts from Marquette Prison to work for him. She had to continually stay on the alert, often having to defend herself from sexual advances. When Mom got older, she found alcohol and began to use it to keep her demons at bay. Later, she has tried to fight the drink by writing, never quite winning the battle.

It appeared to me at first that Mom's goal in life was to write a novel, and for as long as I can remember, she worked on it. The research for her Book was done by phone and hours spent in the city library. The research was a good time for me because I got to go along while she and Dad researched details for The Book. It was a time that developed my love of history and from that a thirst for adventure. I never quenched that thirst, and have enjoyed a varied and exciting life. All of which began because of her novel.

Later, when I was a Marine, I was stationed on a Pacific island. During that time, I was in a gunfight with some intruders who had breached a restricted area. When I wrote home about it, Mom took my letter and turned it into a T.V. script that was picked up by a Canadian network. She was a marvel at viewing life and describing it with the printed word.

Several years later, after Dad died, she read an article in

one of her many magazines about a Detroit car show and that they were having a short story contest. The story had to be about four-wheel-drive vehicles. I had recently purchased a Jeep and took Mom off-roading on my farm, which she enjoyed immensely. Using that experience, she wrote a short story and entered the contest but utilizing a man's name instead of her own. She thought if the judges saw an entry by a woman, they wouldn't consider the entry. She won first prize, and when they met the eighty-five-year-old female author, the delighted judges insisted that Mom use her correct name. They also invited her to the car show and treated her like royalty.

There came a time in my life when I lost almost everything, my marriage, my business, my home, all gone. I was living alone when Mom, now nearly ninety, became bedridden. Her mind was still sharp, but getting around by herself could be a dangerous proposition for her. I moved in and began taking care of her.

Mom was still writing her novel. She would read parts of it to me, and I would comment. During this time, she saw how stressed I was, and she began encouraging me to write. "You've done lots of interesting things in your life," she would say. "Write about it." One night I sat down at my computer, and I started a story. It began to flow, and I typed for hours. My troubles seemed to disappear as men and women I had met, and the smells and sounds of foreign lands became a work of fiction. One evening I brought My Book to Mom.

She was now spending all of her time in bed, doing crossword puzzles and writing. Propped up in bed, she wore reading glasses that made her eyes look huge. Next to the bed, there was a table on wheels that could be raised with a crank. I would crank it up and center it over her hips so she could read, write, or take meals. One night I placed a box with My Book in it next to her.

She looked down at my four hundred page endeavor. "What's this?" She asked.

"I've been writing," I told her.

"Who typed all of this?"

"I did, on my computer."

Mom looked at me as if I were growing snakes out of my head. "I was wondering if you would take a look," I asked her.

It took her several days, but she read it, the whole thing. When she had finished, she picked up a stack of the pages and said, "My God, you even have a dog in it!" Then she began to point out my errors. I quickly felt anger well up in me and became defensive as she pointed these things out.

Stopping, she looked at me with those enormous eyes, "Do you want to learn, or don't you? If you do, then you'd better toughen up. You have a good story here, but a publisher will take one look at it and toss it in the wastebasket." It took a while, but I managed to "toughen up," and she began to teach, and I began to learn. It seemed our lives had come full circle, except now together we were up into the wee hours, writing, talking, remembering. At ninety-four, Mom died.

She never got to see my Book in print, and she never finished her novel. I don't think she ever intended to. It was her way of dealing with her demons. The Book, untitled, hundreds of unnumbered, handwritten and typed pages, is in a box in my closet. Sometimes, like now, I remember, and I can hear the keys of her Royal, and I imagine her alone in that dark room working on The Book.

Christmas For a Moment

I received several emails about a poem I'd written.
    They came from names I knew, faces I'd
    forgotten.
As I looked and found each in the high school
    yearbook, memories came flooding back
And as I searched, music began to play in
    my head
The music was of Christmas, Silver Bells and
    Bing Crosby being home for the Holidays
Crowds of Christmas shoppers wearing boots,
    bundled against the cold traveling store to
    store giving cheerful greetings to young
    and old
I could hear the buzzing wheels of cars on
    Saginaw Street the slushy red bricks
    reflecting the holiday lights
I smelled the caramel corn and heard the ringing
    bells of Salvation as red-nosed volunteers,
    pled help for those with need

Mitten hands fumbling coin into the pot,
receiving a smile and best wishes then
rushing off thankful for their lot
I was a kid in Flint, the thrill of Christmas-past
mine to have again, if only for a moment

A Dream

Everyone has a dream. It may start when you're
young when you begin to see the world for
the first time and how big that world is and
how damned exciting it is. It can start with
movies, T.V., or when your Dad or mom tells
you tales of when they had a dream.

Life has always excited me, bugs, things in the
dark, I was so curious, I didn't know that I
had a dream. Then one day I was getting a
haircut and Bill, the barber, asked me, "So
John, what are your plans.

"Plans," I asked?

"You know when you get older."

Without any conscious thought, I said, "I want to
be a Marine."

Bill stopped cutting my hair, his arms extended
above my head, a comb in one hand, scissors
in the other. The sleeves on his shirt rolled to
his forearm; I could see his Black Panther

*tattoo. Bill had just returned from the
Korean War.*

*Bill said, "There's plenty of time, John, you're not
even sixteen yet."*

*That was fifty-six years ago, and forty-nine years
since I got out of the Marine Corps, a kid's
dream, my dream, which has guided me my
entire life.*

We Were Indians

We were Indians once our class of fifty-nine
We wore our red and black with pride
Our warriors had done us proud
Then on a day of Thanksgiving, our red and
*   black was challenged*
It was that Northern Tribe cross-town all dressed
*   in gray and red*
We gathered around the field of battle to cheer
*   our warriors on*
While opposite the Northern Tribe taunted,
*   "They'd already won!"*
Then the cymbals and the brass began, and a
*   mighty roar went up*
Upon the field came our Indian
Tremewan would lead us as his family had done
*   for years.*
Then a momentary silence as both sides held their
*   breath*
A whistle blew the signal that the battle would
*   commence*

We watched in awe as that prize we sought rose
into the air
While at the end of the field stood a small but
powerful man
An Indian named Moses grabbed the prize, and
then he ran
Both tribes stood in disbelief as Moses dodged
and spun
He ran downfield through the mud and muck, his
eye upon the goal
Then a warrior from the Northern Tribe
challenged his mighty stroll
Oh it did look like the end as the Northern pulled
our warrior down
But through a wave of mud and grass Moses slid
cross that line
Amid the sounding brass, the Class of Fifty-nine
sent up a cheer
Tremewan, the warrior, began our victory dance
For we knew the day was ours, that year in 58

Lessons Learned

I'm with my Dad in Wolverine, Michigan, it is February 1954, and it is my thirteenth birthday. For my birthday I got a pair of logger-boots that smell of "Bear Grease" that under the direction of my father, I applied the night before. The grease waterproofs the leather. The boots are still warm from sitting on the heat register all night so that the grease would melt into the leather. Dad has instructed me to stuff the boots with newspaper when I come back in to absorb any moisture in the boots. When they are dry, I'm to apply more grease to keep them soft.

My Dad and I are in a wooded area not far from where he grew up. Jake is with us; he is a brown, medium-sized dog that is giddy about going hunting. He sits, stands, runs, and paws at my Dad, anxious to get going.

Dad removes a single-shot, four-ten gauge shotgun from the trunk of the car. It is the same shotgun he used when he was a kid. He breaks it open and inserts a red and copper shell and then snaps it shut. Jake is beside himself now, running in low circles, kicking up the snow. Dad leads us away from the car to an open area and stops. I'm excited. I'm ready to hunt.

Silently, Dad, with his fingers extended, sweeps his arm forward towards the woods. Jake bounds off into the woods and disappears. I'm thinking, "Let's go; Jake is way ahead of us." I look up at Dad, who is facing the woods when I hear Jake's bellow. Dad smiles and cocks the hammer back on the shotgun and then places the stock-butt on his hip. Now Jake is crying long and loud; he's getting closer. Dad moves the gun from his hip to a ready position.

A snowshoe rabbit burst into view, in an instant, the shotgun is at Dad's shoulder, and the report echoes through the woods. The rabbit does a flip into the air then lands in the snow. Just as Dad lowers the shotgun, Jake comes into view. He streaks towards the now still rabbit, stops, sniffs, and then pushes the rabbit with his nose. Jake sits down and looks at Dad.

Dad and I approach the rabbit and Jake. Dad picks up the rabbit by the hind legs and holds up for Jake to see. Dad pets him on the head and scratches him behind his ears, all the time telling Jake what a good dog he is. I swear there's a smile on Jakes' face.

It's dark when we get back to Grandma's house. Dad hands me the rabbits and the shotgun to carry in. Then he goes to the backdoor of the car, opens it, reaches in and picks up Jake.

Jake is exhausted; the areas around his eyes are slightly swollen from running through weeds and brambles. His feet are sore from a long day of hunting. He doesn't struggle in Dad's arms as I rush ahead to open the door for them.

Inside, Dad places Jake next to a floor register as Grandma brings in a blanket. Dad spreads the blanket on the floor, folding it to cushion Jake. Dad moves Jake to the blanket then examines his feet for cuts. When he's sure there are none, he gets water and food and sets it close by.

I go out onto the back porch where I left the rabbits. Grandma brings me a huge bowl of saltwater. I begin to clean the rabbits and then place them in the water. Later, I take them into the house and put the bowl of rabbits into the refrigerator.

I peel off my boots and stuff them with an old newspaper as Dad instructed, and I place them by Jake on the heat register.

I get the shotgun, and under Dad's watchful eye, I clean it. The smell of burnt powder and "Hoppie's Gun Oil" is a smell I'll always remember. That and the lessons learned that day.

Woofer-D and the Motor City Kitty

It was a winter day in 1944, when Woofer-D and Motor City Kitty arrived at our house, nestled in the pockets of my father's overcoat. I was about three and delighted when they poked their heads up and out of Dad's pockets to greet me.

Woofer-D was a "get-the-last-word-in" kind of dog. It's how he got his name. Anyone coming to the door or slamming a car door, Woofer would, "Woof!" When told he had woofed enough, there would be a pause, and then softly, "Woof." If you gave him the last word (woof), he would be silent, but he is prepared to go on indefinitely. The "D" stood for dog.

Woofer was a black, fifty pound, unknown breed with a stubby tail and long hair that covered his body and hung over his eyes. He loved mud puddles and, after luxuriating in one, knew to head directly to the basement for a bath when he entered the house. He loved to play and was every boy's dream dog. I'm sure had we lived in California rather than Flint, Michigan, he would have become a star.

Motor City Kitty was large, brown, short-haired Tabby-cat with black stripes. His eyes were golden, and he was a brilliant cat. Because we lived in Flint, Michigan, and his singing voice was loud and smooth, like a good engine, he became The Motor City Kitty. I couldn't pronounce his name and dubbed him Keen. Keen would remain his name.

For the first five years of my life, WWII was on, and things were very tight financially for our family. We lived in a two-bedroom, condemned house with a potbellied stove in the living room. I never did find out why we were able to live in a condemned house, but we did. It was in this house that Woofer and Keen became family heroes.

Keen was the first hero, and it was a story told to me many times over the years. It was early one morning when my mother found a huge sewer rat lying under my crib. It was dead. Close by lay Keen. He had been in a vicious fight, which left him severely wounded in the face and side. It appeared the rat had tried to get into my crib, and Keen had stopped him.

"I don't care how much it costs," my mother told Dad, "You take him to the vet." Dad wrapped Keen up in a blanket, and off they went to the vet. Mom said the vet was so impressed with Keen that he cut his fee. Woofer, who had been out all night, was noticeably concerned about Keen, and for days stayed close, until his buddy was back on his feet.

A year later, Woofer and my Dad teamed up to once again to save the family. The house was old, and the wiring terrible. About two o'clock, one-morning, Woofer began to bark and race about the house. He scratched at the bed covers woofing then running away barking. Dad got up to find smoke seeping from one of the walls. Mom said Dad smashed his fist through the wall and found the fire and the arcing wires. He reached inside and ripped the wires out, while mom called the fire department. I slept through the whole thing and didn't know about it until the kids across the street told me.

Mom was on the phone one day when Woofer went to the door to let her know he wanted out. Mom let him out and continued talking. Soon Woofer wanted in, and Mom obliged. Soon he was at the door again wanting out, and Mom opened it. He was at the door again, scratching to come in when Mom hung up the phone, "What is he up to," she wondered.

Woofer went straight to the kitchen, and before Mom could get there, he headed to the door to go out. Spotting a bit of color through the hair around his mouth, Mom lifted the hair away and found an orange. Woofer had been taking the oranges from the bag, sitting on the kitchen floor, outside, and burying them in the Victory garden. Mom let him out, and then followed him to his stash and retrieved the oranges. We never could figure out why he did it.

After the war, things changed for our family, and we moved to a nice neighborhood. The house was a two-bedroom with doors on the rooms and one in the hallway. Shortly after the move, we began to see just how smart the Motor City Kitty was.

Cats just know when people don't like them. Mom had such a friend who was not fond of cats. Every time she visited our house, Keen made it a point to jump up onto her lap. Mom decided that the best way to deal with this was to put Keen in the bedroom and close the hall door.

Mom and her friend were chatting when they heard the rattling of the doorknob in the hallway. While the two watched in amazement, the door opened and out stepped Keen. He looked about the room, and then, with purpose, he walked directly to the visitor and jumped up onto her lap. Mom was coming to the rescue when her friend held up her hand. "It's his house, she said, "He's fine, please let him stay."

One weekend while we were on an overnight trip, Keen was left in the house by mistake. Woofer was outside, but Keen had no way out, and as an outdoor-indoor cat, had no litter box. Mom was concerned. When we returned, we found him sleeping on my bed in a sunbeam.

While Mom frantically searched the house for Lincoln Logs, Dad discovered that Keen had used the toilet while we were gone. From then on, we left the lid up, but he never did learn to flush.

One summer day, a boy of about ten came to our door and knocked. Mom could see a man in a car parked at the curb, and Woofer was on the porch next to the boy. "Ma'am is this your dog," the boy asked.

"Why yes, his name is Woofer."

"My Dad said that if you would sell him, I could buy him. I've saved ten dollars."

"Well, I'm sorry, but you see, he already has a little boy who would miss him."

The boy thought that over for a minute, and then petted Woofer on the head and left. Mom opened the door, and Woofer came in.

My father was a musician and had a band. After playing, he would return home in the early morning hours. The Motor City Kitty loved my Dad and would follow him around the house, and when allowed, sleep with him. When left outside, on the night's Dad played in the band, Keen would climb the tree across the street and get on the roof of Mister Gray's house. When Dad came home, the Cat would begin to yowl, waking everyone up. Dad, dressed in his suit, would get our extension ladder and go across the street to get Keen. Keen would begin purring at the sight of Dad.

Dad would be on the ladder, feeling like an inept second-story man, when the bedroom window opened. "That you, Mister Wood," Mister Gray would ask.

"Yes sir, sorry we left the cat out."

"Okay," he'd say, "Good night."

Mortified, Dad would retrieve the singing Motor City Kitty from the roof. It became my job to be sure Keen was in the house the night's Dad Played in the orchestra.

Years later, I joined the Marines. While stationed in Guam, I received news that Woofer-D had died, he was eighteen. Mom said he'd developed a heart condition, and he couldn't climb the steps to and from the porch. Dad, now retired, would carry Woofer outside twice a day. Keen grieved a long time after Woofer died.

One afternoon, three years later, Mom found Keen curled up in a sunbeam on my bed. He had died in his sleep. He was twenty-one.

That was nearly fifty years ago. Since then, Mom and Dad have passed, and I'm the only one left who remembers Woofer-D and The Motor City Kitty. They were our friends. They were family.

Apparition Swamp

As Olin slipped and slid past the moonlit swamp, his skin broke out in a cold sweat. His stomach suddenly forced yellow bile up into the back of his throat and then rocketing between his teeth and past his lips. Olin's legs weakened, and then he wilted slowly to the ground. The small sharp stones and twigs on the bank of the swamp poked and stabbed his cold, clammy skin.

The gray, greasy muck of the swamp's bank smelled of dead and decaying amphibians. Olin tried to get to his knees. The sound of falling water stopped him, and he looked towards the moonlit swamp and the source of the falling water. An odor of rotten eggs filled the air as something, something large and black, began splashing in Olin's direction. Fear forced Olin's heart to beat so fast his body began to sweat blood. With a massive, painful convulsion, Olin soiled himself. "Never go near Apparition Swamp at night," his Paw had warned him over and over. But Olin knew if he were late getting home, his Paw would whip him. So ignoring his father's warning, he had taken the shortcut home past Apparition Swamp.

Though the apparition appeared to have no form, its large, thick upper portions moved like the shoulders of a man. The swamp water churned as the vile thing swiftly moved towards Olin, who no longer had the strength to take flight. As the cold steel-like grip of the thing grabbed Olin's leg, Olin remembered something else his Paw had told him, "There ain't no worse death than being eaten alive." Olin tried to scream, but his mouth filled with the acrid black water of Apparition Swamp.

A Soldier's Dream

I saw her through a window; she was dancing
Slender, her arms outstretched, her chin held high
But I didn't have the time to stare before she
was gone
My truck moving towards the frightening
unknown of war
But in that fleeting moment, I stored her image in
my mind
And later, if I were lonely or afraid
I would close my eyes, and she would come
And together we would dance in the moonlight

Memories and Red Snow

Carl squinted into the mirror, a spot of toilet paper stuck on his chin, soaking blood from the razor cut. His eyes dropped to the thin white scar on his throat. It, too, had been a razor cut, made not by a shaking hand with a safety razor, but a straight razor in the skilled hands of an East German assassin. It'd taken more than a spot of paper to stop the bleeding.

Dianna had killed his attacker before he could complete the cut. She'd stopped the bleeding as flakes of snow swirled in her black hair.

"It's okay," she had whispered. "It's okay."

But when she needed him, he wasn't there for her.

In Paris, she was to meet the Russian, but he had set a trap. Carl was her back-up, and when he saw the hidden gunman, he ran to save her. But Carl's leather shoes slipped, and he fell on the snow-slickened cobblestones. The gunman shot her, and both he and the Russian moved away.

Later, Carl found them, and his revenge was terrible, but it meant nothing. She was dead, and all Carl had left was the haunting memory of her words.

"It's okay; it's okay."

Pulling a towel from the rack, he dried his face.

"Maybe I'll grow a beard," he thought.

From the clothes basket, Cat watched with blue eyes. Carl smiled and tossed the towel onto Cat. For a moment, Cat was still, but soon his head popped out, then he jumped from the basket. Cat, stretched, twisted, and quickly licked a spot on his back. Finished, Cat sat, his back turned to Carl.

"You, Cat! Look at my pants, your hair!"

Carl held the black pants up for Cat to see the swirls of white hair. But Cat walked from the room, his tail held high like an expressive middle finger.

Carl, using several wraps of scotch tape wrapped around his fingers, began removing the cat hair from his pants. Finished, Carl held the pants up and examined them. Satisfied, he pulled them on, using the bed's footboard for balance. Then sitting on the edge of the bed, he pulled on a sock. Above the ankle were a band of discolored skin and a white puckered scar. "Cairo," he thought. We'd just started working together. Dianna, such a plain Jane, just right for our world because no one ever looked twice at her. 'But I did, he thought, 'and then I couldn't look away.' Pulling on his sock, Carl covered the scar.

Carl's apartment was small, just large enough for his books, a T.V., and a recliner where he read and watched the news. Cheap black picture frames with photos from the past lined the walls. Carl didn't look at them anymore.

He and Cat just watched the news. But sometimes Carl would long for the sounds and smells of the job, the rush of adrenalin and her, Dianna. 'When you're young, you think it'll last forever,' he thought.

"But forever isn't as long as it used to be, eh Cat?

Well, I'm going for my walk. You watch over things while I'm gone." Cat ignored him.

The black winter morning was freezing, making the exhaust from the cars hang in the crisp air, moisture dripping from cold tailpipes. Snow and the cold air formed halos around the streetlights.

Carl still moved well, though sometimes he'd get a knot in his foot. He'd broken it when he was a kid. He had fallen out of a tree playing army. The thought brought back memories of his boyhood friend Harold and his older brother Jim when drafted, was sent to Korea. When Jim came back, he wouldn't talk about the war. But in the summer, when Jim wore a short-sleeved shirt, there was the scar. It ran from the crook of his arm to his shoulder. "A Chinese bayonet," Harold told Carl. Harold overheard his Dad tell someone. But Jim, he never talked to them about it.

There was something about that scar, and when he was old enough, Carl joined the Marines. Later, Carl was recruited for other things, things that made Carl understand why Jim hadn't talked about the war. The thoughts of Jim and the war brought back memories of Dianna, "It's okay," she'd said, "It's okay."

Carl watched the kids on their way to school, walking in groups, talking loudly, pushing, being kids. Head down, Carl moved through the slush, glad for his new waterproof boots with the deep treads. Carl's eyes flicked from side to side, scanning the street, a habit acquired from years of tradecraft. To the world, just an older man bent by age and the cold. Only another professional, looking for him, might have spotted it.

Moments later, Carl was the only one who saw it coming, the black low-slung car with the tinted windows. The back window was down, with a hand pointing at Carl's side of the street. School kids were gathered in front of a small grocery store drinking Mountain Dew and smoking. Carl knew some were gang members by the clothes they wore.

Then the muzzle of an AK-47 suddenly replaced the hand in the car window. 'It's a hit, gang war,' thought Carl. In Carl's mind, it was Paris again, and Carl began to run, "Gun!" he yelled, "Gun, get down, get down!"

Carl ran towards the kids, pointing and yelling. Some ran, others fell to the ground, then the shooting began. Kids screamed as the bullets knocked holes in the brick walls and windows.

A girl stood frozen by fear, her mouth open, a silent scream stuck in her throat, her eyes black as buttons. Carl saw her.

His legs pumping, his new boots dug into the slush, propelling him towards the girl. The bullets raced him.

The girl's scream was knocked from her as Carl's weight drove her down to the wet sidewalk. Like a black serpent, the car fishtailed up the street.

For a moment, there was a vacuum of silence, then sobbing mingled with anxious words of concern. Someone rolled Carl away from the girl; her white blouse blood-soaked.

"The girl's been hit! Call an ambulance." someone yelled.

"She's all right, I think. It's the Old Man. It's his blood."

"Jesus, did you see that? Hadn't been for him, those gang bangers would have shot us all."

The girl's mother had been in the store when the shooting started. She nearly swooned at the sight of her child covered in blood.

"She's all right, lady, the blood's not hers. It's the Old Guy. I think it's his."

Distant sirens announced the approach of the police. The mother, first frantically checking her child, knelt next to Carl. Snow swirled about the snow on the ground, colored by the red neon from the store.

Carl smiled up at the face of Dianna, "it's okay," they heard him say, "it's okay."

Instantly

She died instantly, the emergency room doctor told me, but she didn't. Here I sit, in the dark, two years later, and Loretta, my wife, the love of my life still lives. I can smell her golden hair and feel the soft warmth of her breath upon my face. Sometimes she comes to me in my dreams so real that when I awake, I can barely stand the shock of not touching her. Yet I eagerly seek her again each night, forgetting the pain the morning brings, for one more night with her.

I read somewhere that a person dies three times. The day they die, the day they are buried, and the last time we speak their name. Loretta may live a long time for sleeping in the next room is her living image. At ten, Kaylie still has real memories of her mother. Sometimes at night, just before she sleeps, Kaylie will ask me about her mom. I take her with me to the time I first met her mother or told her about the day we were married. I speak of our joy at her birth and how her mother loved every minute she had with her.

The three of us live together, two of us keeping the third

alive in our hearts. With luck, Loretta will live a long time; there might be grandchildren, perhaps even great-grandchildren, and Loretta's name will be spoken over and over. Life's little gift, for no one, dies instantly.

Dear reader,

We hope you enjoyed reading *The Ramblings of John W Wood*. Please take a moment to leave a review, even if it's a short one. Your opinion is important to us.

Discover more books by John W. Wood at

https://www.nextchapter.pub/authors/john-wood-historical-fiction-author-united-states

Want to know when one of our books is free or discounted? Join the newsletter at

http://eepurl.com/bqqB3H

Best regards,

John W. Wood and the Next Chapter Team

Lightning Source UK Ltd.
Milton Keynes UK
UKHW022033180121
377284UK00004B/699

9 781034 244387